Karen's Easter Parade

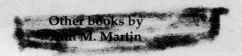

Little Sister

Karen's Easter Parade
Ann M. Martin

Illustrations by Susan Crocca Tang

A
LITTLE APPLE
PAPERBACK

SCHOLASTIC INC.
New York Toronto London Auckland Sydney
Mexico City New Delhi Hong Kong

ISBN 0-590-52521-2

Copyright © 2000 by Ann M. Martin. Illustrations copyright © 2000 by Scholastic Inc. All rights reserved. Published by Scholastic Inc. THE BABY-SITTERS LITTLE SISTER, LITTLE APPLE PAPERBACKS, and associated logos are trademarks and/or registered trademarks of Scholastic Inc.

12 11 10 9 8 7 6 5 4 3 2 1   0 1 2 3 4 5/0

Printed in the U.S.A.   40
First Scholastic printing, April 2000

The author gratefully acknowledges
Gabrielle Charbonnet
for her help
with this book.

Karen's Easter Parade

Mommy's Surprising Announcement

"Hello, hello, hello!" called Mommy as she opened the front door.

"Mommy!" Andrew and I cried. (Andrew is my little brother.) We raced to the door.

"Would you help me with these bags, please?" said Mommy. She handed Andrew and me each a grocery bag. We carried them to the kitchen.

"Hi, Merry," said Mommy.

"Hi, Lisa," said Merry. Merry is our nanny. She helps take care of Andrew and me while Mommy is at work. "Did you have a good day?"

"I had an excellent day," said Mommy as she put a fresh gallon of milk in the fridge. "In fact, I had an extra-specially good day."

"Wow! What happened?" I asked. Maybe Mommy had met someone famous. Or maybe she had won a contest!

"I have some fun news," said Mommy. "But I want to wait until Seth is home. I will tell everyone over dinner."

"Oh, boy!" I said loudly. "It is a million years till dinnertime." (Mommy did not remind me to use my indoor voice, so I knew she must be in a very good mood.)

Mommy smiled at me. "I know it is hard to be patient, but I cannot tell you anything until Seth is home."

I sighed and started to put cans on a shelf in the kitchen. Mommy was right. It is very hard to be patient — especially for me. But I would try.

You are probably wondering who Seth is. He is married to my mommy. That makes him my stepfather. And now you are probably wondering who I am. Well, hold your horses. I will tell you.

My name is Karen Brewer. I am seven years old and live in Stoneybrook, Connecticut. I have blonde hair and blue eyes and freckles on my nose. I will tell you more about me later. And, believe me, there is plenty more to tell!

While Mommy read the day's mail, I helped Merry set the dinner table. Getting dinner ready was not going to make Seth come home from his workshop any earlier. (Seth is a carpenter who makes beautiful furniture.) But it felt like it would.

I rushed back and forth from the kitchen to the dining room, putting out forks, knives, and spoons. We were going to have spaghetti. Because everyone in my little-house family eats spaghetti in a different way, everyone got a different combination of utensils. Mommy cuts her spaghetti into pieces with a fork and knife. Seth twirls it on his fork against a spoon. I eat mine long,

3

but I do not twirl it against a spoon. (I use the plate.) And Mommy cuts up Andrew's for him and he eats it with a spoon. So here is who got what:

> Mommy — fork and knife, no spoon
> Seth — fork and spoon, no knife
> me — fork, no spoon or knife
> Andrew — spoon, no fork or knife

It was hard to keep all that straight. But I did. Plus, I remembered to set out napkins and glasses. And by the time I had done all that — Seth arrived!

Merry went home and my family sat down to dinner.

"Mommy, now will you tell us your fun news, please?" I begged.

"All right, Karen," said Mommy, smiling. "I can see that the suspense is killing you. Well, today I got a phone call from Ellen." Ellen is Mommy's sister. "She and her family will be celebrating Easter with us here in Stoneybrook."

"Yippee!" I shouted, leaping out of my chair. This was a fabulous surprise. I started dancing around the dining room. "Diana is coming! Diana is coming!" I sang.

Diana Wells is my cousin. She is my age. We are like twins. We had a magical adventure together one summer in Maine. I love Diana!

Mommy and Seth laughed.

"Okay, Karen, settle down," Mommy said. "I have more to say."

"More?" I gasped. I put my hand on my chest.

"Diana will be spending a whole week with us by herself," said Mommy, "before the rest of her family arrives. And she will be here in just two days."

"Two days!" I shrieked. "Two days from now!"

This time Mommy did say, "Indoor voice, Karen." But she said it with a smile on her face.

My Two Families

Now I will tell you more about myself. A long, long time ago, when I was little, I lived in a much bigger house. I lived there with Mommy, my daddy, and Andrew. Mommy and Daddy did not get along. One day they decided that they did not want to be married to each other anymore even though they loved Andrew and me very much. So they got divorced. Mommy and Andrew and I moved to a little house. Daddy stayed in the big house. (It is the house he grew up in.)

After awhile Mommy met a nice man named Seth Engle, and they got married. Seth came to live in the little house with us.

Then Daddy met a nice woman named Elizabeth Thomas, and they got married. So Elizabeth is my stepmother. She moved into the big house with Daddy.

In my little-house family, there are four people and four pets. The people are Mommy, Seth, Andrew, and me. The pets are Emily Junior, my pet rat; Bob, Andrew's hermit crab; Midgie, Seth's dog; and Rocky, Seth's cat.

In my big-house family, though, there are more people than pets. The people are Daddy, Elizabeth, Andrew, and me. But that is not all! Elizabeth was married once before, and she has four children. They are Sam and Charlie, who are so old they go to high school; Kristy, who is thirteen and is the best stepsister in the world; and David Michael, who is seven like me. Plus, there is my little sister, Emily Michelle, who is two and a half. Daddy and Elizabeth adopted her from a faraway country called Vietnam. Finally, there is Elizabeth's mother, Nannie, who came to live at the big house to help take care of everyone. Whew! Nannie has her hands full, with all those people! And I have not even told you about the pets yet.

First there is Shannon, David Michael's huge Bernese mountain dog puppy. Then there is Pumpkin, our black cat; Crystal Light the Second, my goldfish; and Goldfishie, Andrew's goldfish. And when Andrew and I are at the big house, Emily Junior and Bob are with us too.

Andrew and I like spending time with both of our families (and they like spending time with us). So we switch houses almost every month. We spend one month at the little house, then one month at the big house. At first it was confusing, but we are very used to it now. The trick is to have two of all our most important things, and to keep one at each house. For instance, we each have two bicycles, one at the big house and one at the little house. I have two favorite stuffed cats, two toothbrushes, two sets of pajamas, and even two pieces of my special blanket, Tickly.

And of course Andrew and I have two mommies, two daddies, two cats, two dogs . . . the list goes on and on. Because we have two of so many things, I gave us special names. I call us Andrew Two-Two and Karen Two-Two. (I thought of that name after my teacher, Ms. Colman, read my class a book called *Jacob Two-Two Meets the Hooded Fang*.)

I also have two best friends. Hannie Papadakis lives across the street and one house over from the big house. Nancy Dawes lives next door to the little house. Hannie and Nancy and I call ourselves the Three Musketeers, and our motto is "All for one and one for all."

Once I saw a movie called *The Four Musketeers*. It was about the Three Musketeers and their new friend, who became the fourth Musketeer. Could that happen to us

now? Could Diana become the fourth Musketeer?

I hoped so, and I was almost sure it would. I loved Diana so much that of course my friends would too.

Big Plans

"You will love Diana," I said to Hannie and Nancy.

It was Friday morning. We were playing on the playground at Stoneybrook Academy before school began. I had been telling my two best friends all about my best cousin.

"I cannot wait to meet her," said Hannie.

"Me neither," said Nancy. "Any friend of Karen Brewer's is a friend of ours."

I smiled.

"What are you guys doing for the holidays?" I asked.

"Hannie is coming to our Passover seder on Thursday night," said Nancy. A seder is a long dinner, with readings and singing and a fun game of find-the-matzoh-bread for the kids. I know, because I have been to seders at Nancy's house before.

"Nancy is coming over to my house for dinner on Easter Sunday," said Hannie.

"Oh," I said. Even though I would be with my favorite cousin on Easter, I suddenly felt left out. Hannie at Nancy's Passover seder, and Nancy at Hannie's Easter dinner — and I was not invited to either. Easter boo and Passover bull-frogs!

You know what? My friends could tell I was upset.

"Oh, Karen," said Nancy. "My mom called your house last night to invite you to the seder. But your mother said Diana was coming to visit, so you could not go."

"My mother invited you to our Easter dinner," said Hannie. "And your mom said the same thing to her."

"So do not think you were not invited," said Nancy.

I smiled. "Okay," I said. I felt much better. I did not mind not going to Nancy's house or Hannie's house. I would be happy with Diana. But I did want to be invited.

"And maybe we can still spend part of Easter Sunday together," said Hannie. "All four of us — the Three Musketeers, plus Diana. There is going to be an Easter parade downtown during the day."

"Really?" I said. "Let's all ask our parents if we can go!"

"Okay," said Nancy. "I saw a parade last year. I hope this one has marching bands, and floats, and people selling cotton candy, and lots of fun parade-y things."

"Me too! It will be a blast!" I said. "An Easter blast!"

Preparing for Diana

That afternoon I leaped off the school bus almost before it stopped. I yelled good-bye to Nancy and burst through my front door. The next day was Saturday, the day Diana would be coming. I had to get ready!

Merry was waiting for me with a snack. I wolfed it down. Then I raced to my room.

First, I cleaned it. Not that it was too, too messy. But I will tell you a secret if you promise not to tell anyone else. Sometimes when Mommy asks me to clean my room, I do not really put all my things away. I shove them under my bed. Or in my closet. Flat things go under the rug. And they stay there. But I did not want Diana to find a bunch of old clothes and game pieces and papers crammed under my bed and in my closet and under my rug. So I dragged everything into the middle of the room, and put it all away. Mommy would be so proud.

One of the things I found under the bed was a T-shirt with the words PACKETT FAMILY REUNION on it. It made me remember when I met Diana. That was in Maine, at Mommy's family reunion. (Mommy was a Packett before she got married.) Everyone there got a T-shirt just like mine.

Diana had flown up from Pennsylvania with her family, and I had driven up with Mommy, Seth, and Andrew. (It was a very long drive. I remember how hard it was to be patient in the car.) When we finally got there, Maine was beautiful, and the reunion was fun, fun, fun!

But the best part of the trip was not the reunion. It was the magic garden that Diana

and I found. Let me explain. In the attic of my aunt Carol's house (that was where we were all staying), Diana and I discovered an old diary that had been written over a hundred years before. It had belonged to a girl named Annemarie, and it told about her summer with her cousin Polly. Annemarie and Polly were just like Diana and me — cousins, and almost like twins. From the diary, Diana and I learned about a magic garden nearby. Using clues (I am an excellent detective), we were able to find the garden. And the most amazing thing was that we found the "memory boxes" that Annemarie and Polly had hidden in the garden wall. They were filled with lockets and pictures and other treasures.

It was definitely one of the best adventures I had ever had. And it all came flooding back when I found the Packett Family Reunion T-shirt underneath my bed. For a long time after I came home from Maine, I had slept in that T-shirt. Then I got a new nightie with a pink bow at the neck. I had somehow forgotten about the T-shirt. Now it was rumpled and dusty and musty-smelling.

I ran downstairs and tossed the T-shirt into the laundry pile. It would be nice and clean and fresh-smelling for the next night, when I would wear it for Diana. Since Diana and I were practically twins, we often thought the same things at the same time. I was sure that Diana would remember to wear hers too.

Diana Arrives (Yea!)

"Do I look nice, Mommy?" I asked. I was wearing a blue corduroy dress, with white socks and black shoes. A matching blue ribbon held up my hair. I started to pull on my coat.

"You look very nice, sweetie," said Mommy.

"Goody," I said. I wanted to look extra-special nice. We were going to the train station to pick up Diana. She was coming all the way from Pennsylvania without her parents.

"Mommy, when can I visit Diana by myself?" I asked in the car on the way to the station.

"Someday, maybe," said Mommy from the front seat. (I knew this meant "Not anytime soon.") "But you know, Karen, Diana is not riding the train all by herself. Her parents hired a chaperone to go with her."

"What is a chaperone?" I asked.

"A chaperone is an older person who can take care of a child and make sure they do not get into any trouble," said Mommy.

"You mean a baby-sitter," I said.

Mommy turned around and smiled at me. "Well, yes," she said. "But chaperone sounds older."

I nodded.

"Diana's chaperone on the train is a college student from Stoneybrook who is coming home for Easter break," explained Mommy. "Diana's parents paid for her ticket, and she agreed to look after Diana on the trip."

"Oh," I said. That sounded like a good plan.

When the train pulled into the station, I

held up a sign I had made out of poster board. It said:

♥ ♥ ♥ ♥ ♥ ♥

WELCOME, DIANA!
OOO XXX OOO XXX

I waved the sign back and forth over my head. People started filing out of the train cars. Then I saw her.

"Diana!" I shouted. "Diana, over here!"

Diana ran toward me. We leaped into each other's arms and hugged tight.

"Karen!" she screamed.

"Diana!" I screamed.

We hugged again, then screamed each other's name again, then hugged some more. I felt so, so happy.

Mommy, Daddy, and Andrew joined us. With them was a teenager in a sweatshirt and a plaid fuzzy jacket. She was dragging a large dark green suitcase and carrying a smaller backpack with animal stickers all over it.

"Karen, this is Diana's chaperone, Deborah," said Mommy.

Deborah said hello to me, and I said hi to her. Then Deborah saw her own parents, who had come to pick her up.

"Here is your backpack, Diana," said Deborah, and she handed it to Diana.

"Okay," said Diana grumpily. "I had not forgotten it, you know. I knew I had left it in the overhead rack. I was planning on going back and getting it."

"Okay," said Deborah. "Do you want your juice box?" She held out a box of apple juice.

"Juice boxes are for babies," said Diana.

Deborah shrugged and smiled at all of us. "Good-bye." Then she ran off to join her parents. I noticed that Diana had not said good-bye to Deborah. (She had not said "thank you" when Deborah gave her the backpack either.)

Hmm.

6

Riding Bikes

As soon as we got home, Andrew and I showed Diana around the little house.

"This is my room," I said. "I cleaned it up especially for you. There is nothing under the bed even. And we are going to set up a cot for you right here, next to my bed. So we can talk at night. Remember how we slept out on the screened porch in Maine?"

Diana nodded and glanced around my room. She did not seem very impressed with how clean it was, or with any of my neat things. But maybe she would like our pets.

So I called Rocky and Midgie and showed Diana Emily Junior in her big cage. Andrew even let Diana hold Bob for a few minutes. Diana seemed to like the pets a little bit.

After lunch it was time for Andrew's quiet time. (Usually he does not fall asleep, so we do not call it nap time anymore.) Since I am seven, I do not have to have quiet time.

"Want to go on a bike ride?" I asked Diana.

"Sure." She did not sound very excited, though. She had not seemed very excited about anything (except hugging me at the train station) all day.

As we rode around the neighborhood, we did not talk very much. Something was bothering Diana. Because I was her best cousin, I could tell these things. I wondered what was wrong. Then I remembered once when I was at overnight camp, and I had felt sad and homesick. Was that how Diana felt now?

"Are you okay?" I asked her.

"Yes," Diana said. "I am fine."

"I mean, if you miss your family and are homesick, I would understand," I said. "Really."

"I said I was fine. I am not homesick. I am a big girl now. I turned eight last month, for your information. I am not a little seven-year-old baby anymore. I am even old enough to ride the train by myself. I did not need a baby-sitter at all."

Diana started pedaling fast and left me behind, looking at her in surprise.

"Diana, come back!" I called after her. "You do not know where you are going. You might get lost!"

"I will not get lost!" Diana yelled back at me. "I am not a baby!"

And she pedaled away even faster.

Well, my goodness. I did not know what I had done wrong. I had only asked if she felt homesick. Why was she mad at me? I started pedaling fast to catch up. Stoney-brook is not a humongous town, but still, Diana could get lost. How would I explain that to Mommy? "Diana, wait!" I called.

Easter Eggstravaganza

I caught up with Diana, worried about what she would say next. But she did not seem to be mad at me anymore. She did not pedal away from me, and the rest of our bike ride was lots of fun. We stopped at a store and bought lemonade and fruit roll-ups. Her favorite fruit roll-up was strawberry — the same as mine.

And that night, when I put on my Packett Family Reunion T-shirt to sleep in, guess who else put on hers? That is right. Diana!

We were like twin cousins again. I decided Diana had just been grumpy earlier because she was tired after her train ride.

On Sunday, Mommy and Seth helped Andrew, Diana, and me decorate Easter eggs. I love decorating Easter eggs.

"Why are we decorating them so early?" asked Diana. "Easter is not until next Sunday."

"We are going to donate these to the Stoneybrook Easter egg hunt on Tuesday," I explained. "The parade is on Easter Sunday, so the Easter egg hunt will be during the week. Kids are all off from school next week, for spring break. So Tuesday is a great day for the hunt."

For the past month, every time Merry needed to cook an egg, she would prick each end with a thick needle. Then she would blow in one hole and the egg would come glooping out the hole at the other end. (It is not easy to do. I tried it once, but I could not blow hard enough.)

Now we had three dozen clean, emptied-out eggshells saved up for the Easter egg hunt. (It is not a good idea to use regular eggs for a hunt because they might go bad outside the refrigerator.) We were going to dye the eggs, glue glitter to them, and stick stickers onto them.

Andrew, Diana, and I divided up the empty eggs among us. Mommy covered the kitchen table with newspaper and set us up with bowls of dye.

"I am going to make my first egg pink," I said. I carefully slipped one of my eggshells into a bowl of red dye. I had to hold it down with a spoon because empty eggs float.

"Mine will be green," said Andrew as he put an egg in some green dye.

"Well, those will be nice enough, I suppose," said Diana. "But I like to make my Easter eggs look extra-special. I will be back in a minute." She ran upstairs to my room.

Diana came back carrying a white crayon and a bunch of watercolor markers.

"What are you going to do with those?" I asked.

"You will see," said Diana.

Diana sure knew how to decorate Easter eggs. She used the white crayon to draw designs on an egg. When the egg was dipped in the dye, the color did not stick to the crayon, leaving the design white. It looked fabulous!

With the watercolor markers she drew fancy designs on her eggs. Then she dipped them quickly in the dye, and the colors ran together in beautiful artistic patterns. Some of them reminded me of the fired clay pots that Merry makes. (Merry is a potter when she is not being my nanny.)

All the while, Diana talked about what she was doing and how her eggs were coming out better than Andrew's and mine. Sometimes I thought Diana was bragging a little too much and talking a little too loudly (Diana's parents remind her to use her indoor voice a lot, just like mine do). But I had to admit that Diana was right. Her eggs really were much fancier and prettier than Andrew's and mine.

The Late, Late, Late Show

That night Diana and I put on our Packett Family Reunion T-shirts again. I brought out a bag of Easter candy that I had bought with my own money. We were going to have a pre-Easter candy feast. We started with marshmallow bunnies. I liked to eat the ears first. So did Diana.

We were allowed to stay up a little later than usual because I did not have school the next day. I felt as if we were having a sleep-over party! I wished that Hannie and Nancy could be with us, but I also wanted Diana to myself. We would have time all week to play with my friends.

Diana and I told some great riddles. Here are a few:

Q: Why did the dinosaur cross the road?
A: Because chickens had not been invented yet.

Q: Why doesn't glue stick to the inside of the tube?
A: It wants out.

Q: Where is the best place to have a bubble-gum contest?
A: A chew-chew train.

We laughed and laughed. It was as much fun as Maine had been. I was so glad Diana had come to spend the week. Finally Mommy opened my door and told us to settle down and go to sleep.

"Even if you two do not have to go to school tomorrow, I have to go to work," said Mommy. "You are keeping me awake."

Wow. We had stayed up past Mommy's bedtime.

Mommy closed the door, and I whispered to Diana, "Good night. Sleep tight."

"You are not going to go to sleep yet, are you?" Diana whispered back.

"Well . . . yes," I said. "Mommy told us to."

"You do not have to listen to her," Diana said. "If we are quiet, she will never know we are awake. We could stay up all night!"

"But — " I started to say.

"Come on, Karen," said Diana. "It will be fun. We are old enough to stay up late."

"Well . . . I am not sure." I could not decide what to do. Part of me wanted to stay awake. And part of me was tired and sleepy. Besides, Mommy had told us to go to sleep. But a third part of me wanted to keep Diana happy. After all, she was my guest.

"Okay, you can be a baby, then," said Diana. She sounded as if she were frowning. "I will stay up all night by myself, if that is the way you feel about it."

"I am not a baby," I said. "I will stay up with you."

So we talked some more. We talked about Annemarie, the girl whose diary we had found in Maine. And we talked about Polly, her cousin. Then we told knock-knock jokes and scary stories and —

"Karen and Diana!" Mommy said, opening the door. She was very angry. "It is almost twelve-thirty. You should have been asleep hours ago. Now, I am going to tell you for the last time, please stop talking and go to sleep!"

She shut the door hard. I heard her footsteps pounding away down the hall.

"Good night, Karen," Diana whispered.

"Good night," I said.

We were quiet for a minute. And then I must have fallen asleep, because the next thing I knew, Merry was opening my curtains and singing, "Wake up, sleepyheads!"

Helping Merry

"And I would like you two to gather towels for the laundry," said Merry.

Diana and I were eating breakfast, our eyes barely open. Merry was asking us to help her with some of the household chores.

Even though I was still sleepy, I tried to pay attention to what Merry was telling me. If I were a grown-up, I would have drunk a big cup of coffee to wake myself up. (Since I am a kid, I hate coffee. It is too bitter.) Instead, I had a glass of orange juice.

Diana's eyes started to droop. She was

eating her cereal with her head propped on one hand.

"Okay, Merry," I said tiredly. "You can count on us."

"Good," said Merry. "I am glad to hear that, Karen. And I am sure that Diana will be a big help to me too. Right, Diana?"

"Hmrmph?" said Diana, her head jerking up.

"Merry asked if you are going to help do chores around the house this week," I said, giggling.

Diana sighed and said, "I guess so."

Now, normally I am not crazy about doing chores. But I knew that Merry was trying to make the house look beautiful in time for our Easter party with Diana's family and my little-house family. And that is what I told Diana.

"I suppose the Easter party will be fun," said Diana. (She seemed a little more awake.) "A little fun, anyway."

"A little fun?" I said. I was shocked! "It will be the most fun party ever."

"Will there be anyone there besides our families?" asked Diana.

"No," I said. "I do not think so. But having our families there will be more than enough fun. There will be yummy things to eat, and Easter baskets, and — "

"If you say so," said Diana.

After breakfast I gathered the towels and put them in the laundry room. Then I tidied my room (again). Then Merry asked us to sweep the front and back porches. Mostly I swept while Diana looked bored.

"Now what should we do?" I asked Merry.

"Um, you need to clean Emily Junior's cage."

So I did. Diana held Emily Junior while I cleaned the cage. I was hoping we could have fun doing chores, but Diana did not seem interested. When I suggested playing Cinderella while we swept, Diana just rolled her eyes. Finally, Diana took out her handheld computer game. She settled on the couch and started clicking.

Even though Diana was right there in the room with me, I felt a little lonely.

"There is going to be an Easter parade on Sunday too, you know," I reminded her.

"Huh?" Diana said, without looking up.

I repeated what I had just said.

"A parade? Really?" said Diana. "That sounds like fun. More fun than a boring old family party, anyway."

I did not argue with Diana about whether our family party was going to be fun. I was just glad she seemed excited about the parade. All the same, I wondered again what was going on with Diana. Sometimes she was fun and we were best cousins. And sometimes she was like a stranger to me.

Egg Hunt

"Hurry, Diana, we are going to be late," I called up the stairs.

"I am coming!" Diana yelled back.

The Easter egg hunt in downtown Stoneybrook was due to start in less than fifteen minutes. We would have to hurry if we were going to arrive on time.

Merry and Andrew were waiting in the car for us when we piled in. It was a beautiful spring morning, chilly and sunny and clear. I snuggled into my jacket and put my hands into my pockets.

"There will be prizes for the ones who find the most Easter eggs," said Andrew, wiggling excitedly.

"What kind of prizes?" asked Diana.

"Candy," said Andrew. "Chocolate bunnies. Marshmallow eggs."

"Yum," I said. I love all of those things. My own private, personal bag of candy had been eaten awhile ago. I was glad I would not have to wait until Easter morning for more treats.

Merry parked the car near the town square, and we dashed to the information booth to get our official egg-carrying baskets. The town square, where the eggs were hidden, was roped off. I saw a bunch of people I recognized, but I could not see Hannie yet. She had said she was coming.

A man walked up onto a little stage and said into a microphone, "Welcome, everyone, to Stoneybrook's annual Easter egg hunt. There will be prizes for the children who collect the most eggs. So that everyone has a chance, children five and under will be given a brief head start."

"Yea!" shouted Andrew.

Merry led Andrew to where a bunch of other little kids were being allowed to pass beneath the rope into the town square. Diana and I had to stay behind the rope.

"Now, begin!" shouted the man at the microphone. "Happy hunting!"

The five-and-unders dashed around the square, finding eggs under bushes, in the long grass, underneath benches. Some of the really little kids walked right past eggs that I could see from all the way behind the rope! The parents were calling instructions and laughing. It was really funny.

"Man! Look at that! We will not have a chance to win, the way the little kids are going," said Diana. She sounded mad.

"It is okay," I said. "Even if we do not win, we will have fun hunting for eggs. And we will have plenty more candy on Sunday. Besides, the kids are so cute."

Right in front of us, a little girl found her first egg, held it up proudly, and said, "Mine egg! Mine egg!" I laughed.

"It is not fair," Diana muttered.

Finally the man at the microphone blew a whistle, and we big kids could start hunting. Diana and I raced through the square. We pawed through bushes, searched beneath the water fountains, and reached up high into trees. We each found some, but not nearly as many as some of the younger kids had.

The egg hunt leader blew another whistle, and it was time to stop searching and start counting our eggs. I had looked around again for Hannie, but decided she had not made it after all. But maybe I could go to her house later.

"Look, look!" cried Andrew, running to Diana and me. "I have a billion eggs!"

"Good for you!" I said. "Let's all count." I tapped each egg in my basket as I counted it. "Hey, here's one of ours!" I cried, holding up an egg that I recognized.

"That was one of mine," said Diana. "It's really cool."

"Anyway, I have seven," I said. "How many do you have?"

"Nine," Diana answered.

"Fourteen," said Andrew. (Diana helped him count.)

"That is pretty good," I said happily to both of them.

"If I had gotten a head start, I would have gotten thirty," said Diana. "I saw a little kid over there who must have twenty."

"Well, it does not ma — " I began, but Diana took my arm and dragged me away from Andrew. She lowered her voice to a whisper.

"Hey, Karen, here is an idea. If you give me all your eggs and pretend that you did not find any, I might have enough to win. Do you want to go in with me? I will share the prize with you."

My mouth dropped open. Diana wanted to cheat!

"I do not think that is the right thing to do," I said. "And besides, if we go in together, we will have more than Andrew, and he will lose his prize."

Diana frowned. "So?"

46

Well. I could not believe that Diana did not see how mean that would be. So I decided to believe she was just kidding me.

"Ha-ha," I said. "That would be pretty funny. Now come on. The judges are counting the eggs. We have to show them our baskets." I ran off quickly, before she could try to talk me into being a meanie-mo.

Well, it turned out that Andrew won third place! His prize was a box of chocolate bunnies. If Diana and I had cheated, Andrew would have come in fourth and gotten just a marshmallow chick. I was very glad we had not cheated.

Besides, Andrew shared his chocolate bunnies with Diana and me, because he is generous and kind. I made a big show out of praising him in front of Diana.

Diana did not say anything, but she seemed grumpy.

Still, she managed to eat the chocolate bunny Andrew had given her.

Sam the Easter Bunny

We were standing in the middle of the town square, finishing off our chocolate bunnies, when who should join us but Sam, my big-house big stepbrother!

"Hi, Karen! Hi, Andrew!" Sam called.

"Hi, Sam!" I said. "Let me introduce you to my cousin. Sam Thomas, this is Diana Wells."

"Nice to meet you," said Sam.

"Hi," said Diana.

"What are you doing here?" I asked Sam.

"You are a little old for Easter egg hunts, aren't you?"

Sam laughed. "I am a volunteer," he said. "I helped hide the eggs early this morning."

"You did a good job," said Andrew. "But not good enough. I found fourteen!"

Sam laughed. "That is great, Andrew," he said. "Hey, are you guys going to go to the Easter parade on Sunday?"

"Sure," I said. "I love parades. I would not miss it for the world."

"Great," said Sam. "Then I will probably see you there."

"Oh, are you marching?" Diana asked.

Sam gave her a funny look. "No, not marching, exactly," he said. "At least, not any more than anyone else. Promenading, I think, is what people call it."

Diana and I exchanged confused looks. But before we had a chance to ask Sam what he was talking about, he explained.

"Actually, I am going to stand out in the crowd," Sam said. "I will be wearing a bunny suit and collecting money for charity."

"A bunny suit?" I said. "Like the Easter Bunny? That will be so cute. Are you going to have big floppy ears and a fuzzy white tail?"

"Of course," said Sam. "No proper bunny would be seen in public without them."

Diana, Andrew, and I laughed.

"Well, I have to go now," said Sam. "See you Sunday. You girls will have on your best Easter bonnets, won't you?"

For the second time, Diana and I exchanged a confused look.

"Um, sure," I said. "Right."

Sam waved to us and trotted across the square.

"Easter bonnets?" repeated Diana. "Like hats?"

I nodded. "I guess so. Sam said we should wear our best ones. I wonder why."

"Maybe there is going to be a contest for best hat," said Diana.

"That must be it," I said. "Why else would Sam want us to wear our best bonnets?"

"Well," Diana said, very seriously. "Even if I did not win the Easter egg hunt, I know one thing I am going to win — the prize for the most amazing Easter bonnet."

A Bee in a Bonnet

The next morning Diana woke me up early. "Come on, Karen!" she said. "We have to go to the mall and buy hats. Look, I made some sketches of our winning bonnets."

I blinked sleepily. I put on my blue glasses. (I forgot to tell you. Glasses are another thing I have two of. I wear blue ones for reading up close, and pink ones the rest of the time.)

Diana held out a sheet of paper. I looked at her drawings. They showed a couple of gigundoly fancy hats, covered with flowers

and fruit. One of them even showed a bird perched on a twig.

"These are cool!" I said. "It would be so neat if we could find hats with, like, airplanes on them, or hot-air balloons." I sat up in bed, excited. I have an excellent imagination. (Everyone says so.) I could see that Diana and I could have the most amazing Easter bonnets Stoneybrook had ever seen!

"Airplanes?" Diana hooted. "Hot-air balloons? Who ever heard of those things on a hat? No, my idea is much better. Now, we have to go shopping to buy plain straw hats and the stuff to decorate them with. They will be beautiful. They will win the contest. You will see."

"Oh," I said. "Okay. If you say so." I did not see what was wrong with airplanes and hot-air balloons. I have seen pictures of beautiful hot-air balloons. But I wanted Diana to be happy.

That afternoon Merry drove Andrew, Diana, and me to Washington Mall outside of Stoneybrook.

"Your mother asked me to pick up some things at the Party Place for your family gathering on Sunday," Merry said as we entered the mall.

"Oh, who cares about the family gathering?" said Diana. "Our bonnets are much more important than that. Let's find hats first."

I glanced at Merry. By the look on her face I could tell she thought Diana was being rude. But I guessed Merry wanted to be nice to our guest, because she said, "Okay, I suppose we can look for bonnets first."

Well, let me tell you. If you have never shopped for Easter bonnets with my cousin Diana, you do not know how complicated it is. First we went to a department store to look for straw hats. They did not have any good ones. So we had to go to another department store. We did not find any good straw hats there either.

Finally we went to Heads Up, a store that sold all sorts of hats. There we found perfect straw hats for both of us. (Andrew and

Merry were getting tired of looking at hats. I could not blame them.)

Next came the search for plastic flowers. Back to the first department store. Then the second department store. Then the Dollar Store. Then Hank's Hobby Shop. Finally we found a huge selection of plastic flowers, fruit, ribbons, and even plastic birds at Clarke's Crafts.

The hats and materials we bought were really cool. But Merry was not merry. She was mad! We had spent too much time chasing after bonnet stuff. Merry had not had a chance to pick up any of the things we needed for Sunday.

"I guess we will have to come back tomorrow," said Merry. She looked irritated and worn out. Andrew was whining about how he never wanted to see another hat or plastic flower. I felt a little guilty that they were upset. But it did not seem like my fault. And our bonnets were going to be awesome. I could not wait to wear mine to the parade.

As we drove home, Diana talked and talked about how beautiful our hats would look. I wished she would keep quiet until we got home. Merry's face was getting more and more frowny.

Finally, Merry said, "Diana, we spent the whole day searching for hats. It is time to change the subject."

Diana looked amazed. She stared at Merry's face in the rearview mirror. Then she quit talking altogether. I was embarrassed. Merry had never hurt any of my friends' (or cousins') feelings before.

"Anyway," Diana whispered to me, "we will definitely get the prize for best Easter bonnets."

"Um-hmm," I said, looking out the window.

13

Bubble Gum Blues

We were late getting home, so Merry had to rush to get supper ready. Diana and I went upstairs to my room. We spread our hats and flowers and fruit and birds and ribbons all over my bed to admire them.

"No one will have bonnets as amazing as ours," said Diana, picking up a plastic pear. She pretended to bite into it and said, "Mmm, ripe."

I giggled. Then I noticed that she really was chewing on something.

"What's that? Do you have gum?" I asked.

"Oh, sure," said Diana. She reached into her pocket and brought out a box of Bubble Babies. Bubble Babies are little candy-coated pieces of bubble gum shaped like baby animals. All the kids I knew loved them.

She shook the box, and I heard the Babies inside rattling around. "Want some?" she asked.

"Sure!" I said, holding out my hand.

She tapped a couple of Bubble Babies into my hand. I got a pink baby koala bear, a green baby whale, and a blue baby squirrel.

I popped them into my mouth. "Delicious," I said, quoting their television ad. "And nutritious."

"And best of all, free," said Diana, smiling.

"What do you mean?" I asked.

"They did not cost me any money," said Diana matter-of-factly. "I swiped them from the Dollar Store."

I gasped and almost choked on the gum.

60

"You swiped them?" I asked. "Swiped, like stole? Like shoplifted?"

"Yup," Diana said, nodding. "Just slipped them in my pocket and walked out. Easy as pie." She shrugged. "All the older kids do it back home."

Well, I did not know what to say to that one. I thought of the older kids I knew: Sam. Charlie. Kristy. Kristy's friends, who baby-sat for Andrew and me all the time. I knew there was no way that any of them would steal anything. They were too nice. They were too honest. They were my friends.

"The big kids I know do not steal," I said.

"Well, the ones I know do," said Diana. "It is no big deal. It is fun, and you have to be brave and mature to do it." She turned her back on me. Obviously she did not want to talk about it anymore.

Neither did I. I had some thinking to do. I remembered that Diana had wanted to cheat at the Easter egg hunt. And now shoplifting! I knew shoplifting was a really, really awful thing to do. What would Mommy do if she

62

found out? What would my aunt Ellen do? Diana would be in so, so much trouble. I decided Diana was not acting like herself. I was worried about her.

Should I tell a grown-up about what Diana had done? I did not want to get her into trouble. I was not sure what to do.

That night after dinner, Diana called her family in Pennsylvania. The more I had thought about it, the more I believed that the right thing to do was to tell Mommy about the stealing. It would not be tattling, because I would not be doing it to get Diana into trouble. I was worried, and I wanted to help her.

Mommy and I were alone in the kitchen. I was just about to say something when Mommy said, "What a terrible day I had today."

"What happened?" I asked.

"I found out that someone stole one of my nicest necklaces from the craft center," Mommy said.

"That is awful!" Mommy makes necklaces to sell at the craft center where she works. And they are the most beautiful necklaces ever! I could not believe that someone would steal from her. It made me furious.

"It is," said Mommy. "Now I will not be able to sell that necklace. And we could have used the money for our family celebration." Mommy sighed. "Why do bad people have to do things like that?"

I thought about Diana stealing gum from the Dollar Store. "Maybe they are not bad people," I said. "Maybe they are mostly good people who have bad ideas."

"You are probably right, Karen," said Mommy. "Maybe I should not be so upset. Thank you for trying to cheer me up."

Mommy hugged me. I thought about Diana, and my stomach hurt.

Diana's Other Bad Idea

Diana and I spent Thursday morning decorating our hats. To tell you the truth, I did not really want to be around Diana. Then I felt bad that I did not want to be around her. After all, we are supposed to be best cousins.

I had thought and thought about the gum, and still thought I should tell Mommy what Diana had done. But it was not easy. I had not been able to do it. I wished that I could talk to the other two Musketeers.

They are always ready to help their third Musketeer when she has a problem. But I could not talk to them. I did not want them to know such an awful thing about Diana. So I was on the floor in my room with Diana and a bunch of plastic flowers and fruit, even though I was not excited about our Easter bonnets.

Diana and I glued plastic flowers all around the brim of each hat. Above the flowers we bunched plastic fruit — grapes, lemons, limes, apples. We had even bought one pineapple each, to put on the very top. Next we wove ribbons through the flowers and fruits. Finally, as the most amazing thing, we glued our plastic birds onto little twigs that were stuck into one side. Diana's bird was red, like a cardinal, and mine was blue, like a bluebird.

We tried them on and admired ourselves in front of a mirror.

"Fabulous," I said sadly. "We are sure winners."

Diana frowned. "It is a good start," she said. "But it is not quite enough."

"Not enough?" I repeated. "What else could we put on these hats? Real, live Easter bunnies?"

Diana grinned. "That would be good," she said. "But not possible. No, I think we need some more plastic leaves and berries. And even if we cannot have live bunnies on our bonnets, we can have the next best thing. Last night I noticed some pictures of a little white bunny in a magazine. We can cut out the pictures, put them in frames, and stick them on our hats."

"That is a great idea," I said reluctantly. (Why did Diana have to have such good ideas? It was making everything harder.) "But I do not think I have enough money to buy picture frames."

"No problem," Diana said. "Let's ride downtown on our bikes. We can find picture frames there, right?"

"I guess so," I said. "We cannot go by

ourselves, though. Maybe Kristy can go with us. There is a new store called Nikki's Knickknack Shack. They sell practically everything. But I still do not think we have enough money to buy frames."

"We will not have to buy them, Karen," said Diana. "We will do like I did with the gum. We will swipe them."

"In front of Kristy?" I said. "Anyway, stealing is a terrible idea."

"It is not that big a deal, Karen," said Diana. "Like I said, all the big kids back home do it. And we can do it without anyone seeing us. You are not a baby, are you? Are you chicken?"

I did not know what to say. I definitely did not want to help Diana steal. But I also did not want her to call me a baby or a chicken. I decided to change the subject, fast. Maybe Diana would forget about the store altogether.

"I saw my friend Hannie's bike next door in front of Nancy's house," I said. "You have not had a chance to meet Hannie and Nancy yet. Let's go to Nancy's house. We can go to the store later."

Diana shrugged. "Okay. We will get our stuff this afternoon."

No Floats?

We walked to Nancy's house and rang the doorbell. I introduced my best cousin to my two best friends. (I had wanted to have Diana all to myself when she arrived. But now I could use some company!)

"Karen told us about Maine," said Nancy. "That diary sounded really cool."

"Sure, if you like kids' stuff," said Diana. "I am kind of old for diaries and magic gardens now, though. Hey, do you want to come see the bonnets Karen and I are making for the parade on Sunday?"

"Okay," said Hannie. "But you know, about that parade — "

"Our bonnets are going to be the best ever," interrupted Diana. "We decorated them with flowers and fruit and even little birds. I am sure that they are much more beautiful than anything either of you two kids have."

Nancy and Hannie looked at Diana for a moment silently, blinking. I was horrified. My eyes were wide.

"What Diana meant to say — " I started, but Diana cut me off.

"Our bonnets are amazing," Diana said. "The parade marshal will probably ask us to lead the whole parade. We will be up in front of all the marching bands and fire trucks and baton twirlers and — "

"Ha-ha-ha-ha!" Hannie and Nancy laughed out loud.

"Do you two still think the Easter parade is *that* kind of parade?" Nancy asked, guffawing.

"What do you mean, 'that kind of parade'?" I replied. "What other kind of parade is there?"

"My mommy explained that an Easter parade does not mean marching bands and majorettes and floats and stuff," said Hannie, still giggling. "It just means that people dress up in their best clothes and walk back and forth — parading — and talking and having fun. You did not know that?"

I shook my head. "No baton twirlers?" I asked, feeling a little foolish. "No floats?"

"Nope. And we have known for days," said Nancy, looking at Diana. "I cannot believe you two thought . . ." She cracked up all over again.

I looked at Nancy, thinking about how Diana and I had been planning our Easter bonnets all week. I had been so excited when I thought about the marching bands and the baton twirlers and the floats. I had even hoped the people on the floats would throw little chocolate bunnies to the crowd, and Diana and I, in our fancy hats, would try to catch them! Suddenly it all seemed very funny. I grinned, then I smiled, then I giggled, and finally I was laughing hard with my two best friends. "No floats?" I exclaimed. "What kind of parade is this?"

It was great being with my two best friends again.

Then I glanced at Diana. She was not laughing. She was scowling. Her face was red, and she looked angry and embarrassed.

"I knew that all along," she told Hannie and Nancy, jutting out her jaw. "And Karen and I are still going to win the best bonnet contest, and you two little babies will not. You will see."

"We will not see," said Hannie. Now she looked mad too. "Because there is no way we are going to the Easter parade with you, Diana. You and Karen will just have to go by yourselves. Then you can watch us win the Easter bonnet contest."

"Karen, your cousin reminds me of someone in our class," said Nancy. I did not even have to ask who Nancy was thinking about. I already knew what she was going to say.

74

And Nancy said just what I expected. "Diana, you remind me of Pamela Harding!"

I dropped my head into my hands and groaned. My own best cousin reminded my best friends of my best enemy, Pamela Harding. What was I going to do?

Nikki's Knickknack Shack

Well, let me tell you, Diana and I did not stay long at Nancy's house after that. My friends were really mad at Diana, and Diana was really mad at my friends.

I felt caught in the middle. I wanted everyone to like everyone else. I wanted us to be the Four Musketeers. But I could see that, at least for today, it was not going to happen.

Once we were at home again, Diana said we had to go to Nikki's Knickknack Shack now. I still did not know what to do about

Diana's terrible idea, but Diana insisted that we go soon.

I tried to delay a little by calling Kristy. If she could not come with us, we could not go at all. But Kristy answered the phone on the first ring. She was home. She did not have any plans to baby-sit. She agreed to come over on her bike and take us downtown. I had a feeling that something awful was about to happen, and I did not know how to stop it.

We parked our bikes outside Nikki's Knickknack Shack and went inside. I was so nervous that my heart was beating fast.

They had everything at Nikki's. Shoes, shirts, jewelry, little figurines, vases, lamps, fancy pillows, candles. There were even three whole shelves of plastic flowers, plants, and greenery. Kristy headed for the back of the store. She did not ask us much about what we were doing. She had a long list of things to buy for a school project.

Diana and I picked out some leaves that looked like holly, with little red berries attached. (They looked sort of leftover-Christmassy, but that was okay.)

"All right," I said with relief, reading the price tag. "We have enough money for these leaves."

"We still need the picture frames," said Diana.

"But we don't have the mon — " I said, getting upset.

"Karen, I told you before, it will be no problem," interrupted Diana. "You go and pay for this stuff, and I will get the picture frames."

"Kristy might see you! I do not want you to swipe them!" I said in a whisper.

"Okay, I won't. Just leave it all to me," said Diana firmly.

My stomach started to hurt. My whole Easter was being ruined! Diana had been fun for a little part of her visit but she had been awful for the rest of it. She hated my friends, and they hated her. And now she wanted me to help her shoplift.

I thought about the necklace that had

been stolen from Mommy's booth at the craft center. Mommy had been very upset by the theft. She said we could have used the money to pay for the family celebration. I did not want to do to Nikki's Knickknack Shack what someone had done to us.

"Diana," I said, "you cannot steal anything. It is wrong." I crossed my arms over my chest. "I will not help you. And I will tell Kristy if you do it yourself."

The Worst Easter Ever

"Karen, you are making a big deal out of nothing," hissed Diana.

"What if you get caught?" I said. "What do you think Kristy will do? It will not be nothing then."

"I will not get caught," said Diana angrily. "At home we do it all the time, and no one gets caught. Only babies are chicken. Are you a baby, Karen?"

"I am not a baby or a chicken, and I do not steal things from stores!" I said, my voice rising. I did not care if Kristy

heard me. I was just as angry as Diana now.

"Be quiet!" said Diana. "You will get us in trouble."

"You are the one who is going to get us in trouble," I whispered angrily. "Let's just leave. I'll go get Kristy."

I started dragging Diana across the store.

"Let go of me!" said Diana, wrenching her arm away from me.

"Diana, my mommy just had a necklace stolen from her at the craft center," I said. "She was very upset about it, and so was I. And I am not going to let you do that to somebody else!" I stared hard at Diana. She stared hard at me.

I used my final weapon. "I will tell on you if I have to," I said. "I will tell Kristy right now."

Diana did not say anything for a long time. She looked very angry. "You are spoiling my whole trip, Karen Brewer," she said at last. "You are no fun, and you are a baby and a bad host. Let's get out of here."

"Fine!" I said. We dumped our things into

a messy heap on a counter and stomped out the door. We stood outside, not talking. After a minute I went in to tell Kristy we wanted to go.

Then we rode home. We did not say a word the entire way. I was so, so mad at Diana. I did not even want to be best cousins anymore.

I did not tell anyone what had almost happened at Nikki's Knickknack Shack. Not even Kristy. Diana and I were not speaking. I could tell Mommy and Seth were wondering what was wrong, but they did not ask and I did not say. Instead I played with Andrew, helped Merry, and watched TV. By myself.

On Friday Mommy took the day off from work, and I helped her and Merry get ready for our guests. Diana's family would be arriving on Saturday. We needed to do the final housecleaning and set up the guest room for them.

Diana kept to herself while Mommy,

Merry, Andrew, and I worked. Mostly I saw her reading books and magazines. Once, Mommy asked me if Diana and I were fighting. I told her that we sort of were, but I did not tell her what about. (I had decided that, since I had stopped Diana from shoplifting again, I did not need to tell Mommy about the stolen gum.)

I felt a little bad about ruining Diana's vacation. But you know what? She was ruining mine too. And Diana had given me no choice. It was wrong to steal, and I had done the right thing by stopping her. Even if she was mad at me afterward.

After lunch Sam called. He said he was going to be dressing up as the Easter Bunny at Bellair's department store that evening. He wanted to know if Diana, Andrew, and I would like to come downtown and see him.

Andrew and I said yes! yes! yes! At first Diana said that she did not want to. But finally she said yes too.

No Contest?

Seth drove us to Bellair's that night after dinner. Diana and I were still mad at each other, but I think Diana was more mad at me than I was at her. It is very hard for me to stay mad at someone, especially someone who is supposed to be my best cousin.

At Bellair's, we found Sam in the toy department. He was dressed in a big white bunny suit. He had white makeup on his face, and long whiskers stuck to his cheeks. I wished he could dress like that all the time!

A sign said MEET THE EASTER BUNNY. And a line of people was waiting to meet him. Parents were paying to have their kids' picture taken with him. Sam was talking to the children and making them laugh. He was a very good Easter Bunny.

Even though Andrew knew it was Sam in the bunny suit, he still wanted to have his picture taken with the Easter Bunny. Seth asked Diana and me if we wanted our pictures taken. To tell you the truth, I almost did. I thought it would be funny to have a picture of Sam the Easter Bunny and me. But I decided not to. All the kids having their pictures taken were way younger than me.

"No, thank you," I said politely.

"Oh, no way," said Diana, making a face.

So Seth got in line with Andrew to have his picture taken.

Diana and I stood awkwardly together, not talking. Near us was a group of boys.

They looked a little older than us, and they were talking loudly and laughing in an annoying way.

"Ha-ha! Look at those kindergarten babies, having their pictures taken with the Easter Bunny!" one of them said. "How stupid!"

"Can you believe that guy in the rabbit suit?" said another.

"This is the dumbest thing I have ever seen!" said a third.

Now, let me tell you. I was getting really angry at those older boys. If they did not like what they were seeing, they could go away. They did not have to spoil other people's fun. What they were saying was really rude, and I bet Sam could hear them.

I saw Andrew have his picture taken. Seth stopped to talk with Sam, and Andrew headed back to Diana and me.

"Ha-ha-ha!" jeered one of the boys. "Hey, little kindergarten baby!" he called to Andrew. "Did you have your picthah taken wif de big wabbit?" he asked in a pretend-baby voice.

Andrew looked at the boy and frowned. His face turned red.

"Aww! Do not cwy, wittle baby!" said one of the boys.

Well, I was so angry I was ready to explode. I wanted to shout at the boys to shut up. But there were four of them, and only one of me. And they were bigger than me and looked tough too.

I put my arm around Andrew and glared at the boys. I wanted Seth to come back right away so he could make the boys leave. Suddenly Diana bolted from my side. She charged toward the boys.

"What did you say?" she exclaimed. "Did I hear you say something?"

The boys were so taken aback, they just giggled nervously and stared at Diana.

"Do you think it is funny to pick on people smaller than you are?" Diana went on angrily. "Huh, do you? You guys think you are tough? You are not so tough. You are just bullies. Now get out of here! Go away! No one wants you here." She pointed toward the escalator. "Go!"

My mouth dropped open in shock. I did not know what was going to happen. Would one of the boys hit Diana? All of them were bigger than she was.

Then an amazing thing happened. Without saying a word, all four boys turned on their heels. They slunk away, just as Diana had told them to do.

As their heads disappeared down the escalator, Diana called after them, "And do not come back!"

Just then Seth returned. "What was all that about?"

"Diana chased away some bullies!" said Andrew. "She is my hero!"

"She is my hero too!" I added. I could not believe what she had done.

Diana smiled and blushed. "It was nothing."

"Nothing?" I said. "It was about the bravest thing I have ever seen anyone do!"

Andrew hugged Diana around her waist.

"Well!" said Seth. "I certainly missed something!"

"You sure did!" I said.

"Hi, guys," said Sam, joining us.

"Hi, Sam — I mean, Mr. Bunny," I replied. It was so weird to talk to Sam when he looked like the Easter Bunny.

"That is a great costume," I said. "Too bad you will not be able to enter your bunny head in the bonnet contest."

"Bonnet contest?" Sam said. "What are you talking about?"

"You know," said Diana. "That bonnet contest you told us about. On Sunday. During the Easter parade."

"There is not going to be any contest," said Sam, frowning.

"What?" I said. "First no floats, and now no contest?"

"No," said Sam, laughing. "The parade will be a lot of fun, though. Boy, I do not know where you get your ideas from half the time, Karen."

90

Diana and I looked at each other. Oh, my gosh. We had gone through so much with our hats — shopping for them, making them, and practically ending up enemies over them. And it was all for nothing! For a long moment, we stared at each other. The next thing I knew, Diana and I were hugging each other and laughing. We were best cousins again — for now.

An Easter Surprise

"What do you suppose happened to them?" Mommy asked.

It was Saturday afternoon. Diana's parents and little brother were supposed to have arrived on the three o'clock train from Pittsburgh. But they were not on it when we met it at the station. When the train had come and gone with no Wellses on it, we gave up and came home.

"I hope they are okay," said Diana as we walked into the house. She looked worried.

Brrng! The phone rang.

Mommy answered it. When she hung up, she said, "That was your parents, Diana. They are okay. They got mixed up in New York and missed their connection to Stoneybrook. They are renting a car and will be here in a few hours."

Everyone breathed a big sigh of relief.

"They missed their connection?" said Diana. "And they were the ones who hired a chaperone for me! Maybe next time I should hire a chaperone for them."

Mommy giggled and so did I.

Diana's parents and little brother finally arrived at the little house after dinner. Diana teased her parents about needing a chaperone of their own. But I could tell she was glad to see them. She seemed happy for the first time all week.

On Sunday morning I woke early. Diana was still asleep. (She had been up late the night before, working on something at my desk. She had not let me see it.) I crept out of my room alone and went downstairs to search for my Easter basket. Every year the Easter Bunny hides my basket somewhere in the living room. Sometimes under a table. Sometimes behind a chair.

This year I found my Easter basket behind the big potted plant in the corner. I picked it up and carried it to the kitchen. (We are allowed to look at our Easter candy before breakfast, but we are not allowed to eat any until after.)

When I sat down at my place at the kitchen table, I found a second Easter surprise. It was a note from Diana. It was in an envelope that said TO KAREN. PRIVATE AND CONFIDENTIAL! I ripped open the envelope.

Dear Karen,

I know I have been a terrible guest this week. I am sorry. I am not sure why I acted so bad. I knew I was being awful, but I kept on being awful anyway. I think it was because I was embarrassed about having a baby-sitter on the train with me. I did

94

not want you to think I was a baby. So I tried to act grown-up. Instead I was just bossy and mean. I feel terrible about being rude to your friends. They seemed really nice. And I feel even more terrible about stealing the Bubble Babies. I will go to the Dollar Store on Monday and give them the money for the gum. Thank you for not letting me steal anything else. You are a true friend. I hope you accept my apology. I am really, really sorry about this week.

Love,
Your best cousin,
Diana

Underneath the note was a drawing of Diana and me in our Easter bonnets and Packett Family Reunion T-shirts. We were hugging each other, and a big heart was around us. It was about the most beautiful drawing I had ever seen. I sat in the quiet early morning kitchen by myself with my two Easter surprises. I felt gigundoly happy.

20

The Best Easter Ever

Soon Diana came downstairs.

I smiled at her. "I accept your apology," I said.

We hugged for a long time. Yea, best cousins!

Then we looked for Diana's Easter basket. It was behind the recliner.

By the time we returned to the kitchen, Mommy, Seth, and Diana's parents were there. Pretty soon Andrew and Diana's little brother, Kelsey, had found their baskets too. Then Mommy made eggs goldenrod, as she does every Easter. (I love eggs goldenrod. It is fancy eggs in sauce on top of biscuits. Yum!)

I had two helpings, and so did Diana.

The little house seemed full of people laughing and hugging and having a good time. And now that Diana had apologized, I felt happier than I had in a week.

"Hi, Nancy! Hi, Hannie!" I called.

Diana and I were promenading (that is what walking up and down in fancy clothes is called) at the Stoneybrook Easter parade. The streets had been closed to traffic. Practically the whole town was there, dressed in their finest. Many of the women and girls had gigundoly awesome hats. Diana's and mine were two of the best, even if they did not have framed pictures of bunnies on them. (I am sure that if there had been a contest, we would have tied for first place.)

"Hi, Karen!" Hannie and Nancy called to me.

"Um, Karen," said Diana. "I think maybe

I had better go. Your friends do not like me. I will see you later." Diana started to walk away.

Before she could escape, I grabbed her arm. "Do not go, Diana. I am sure that Hannie and Nancy will give you a second chance. They have given me hundreds of second chances."

Diana smiled. "Okay."

Hannie was wearing a beautiful white bonnet with blue bows all over it. Nancy was not wearing a bonnet. She had a disposable camera, and she was taking pictures of all the amazing hats — including Diana's and mine.

"I love your bonnet," said Diana to Hannie. "It is beautiful." She turned to Nancy. "I am glad you were smart enough to bring a camera. I forgot mine."

"Thank you," said Hannie and Nancy.

Diana chewed on her fingernail for a moment. "I am sorry I was such a meanie-mo the other day," she said. "I was in a bad mood, I guess. I hope we can still be friends."

Hannie smiled. "Any friend of Karen Brewer's — " she started to say.

" — is a friend of ours," Nancy finished for her.

"Hey, look!" shouted Diana, pointing. "There goes the Easter Bunny!"

Our heads turned to see Sam in his rabbit suit, hopping down Main Street, handing out candy from a basket.

Hannie, Nancy, Diana, and I waved and hollered, and Sam tossed a handful of candy in our direction.

We scrambled to catch the candy, and I picked up the ones that had fallen to the ground. We were laughing and shrieking. I looked at Diana and she and Hannie pretended to wrestle for a Tootsie Roll. I smiled. We were finally on our way to becoming the Four Musketeers. Yea, Musketeers! Yea, Easter!

L. GODWIN

About the Author

ANN M. MARTIN lives in New York City and loves animals, especially cats. She has two cats of her own, Gussie and Woody.

Other books by Ann M. Martin that you might enjoy are *Stage Fright*; *Me and Katie (the Pest)*; and the books in *The Baby-sitters Club* series.

Ann likes ice cream and *I Love Lucy*. And she has her own little sister, whose name is Jane.

BABY-SITTERS
Little Sister

Don't miss #121

KAREN'S GIFT

I was doing so well that I could not stop. Maybe I would get lucky again. I decided to try one more house. We had some new neighbors and I did not know if they had any pets. I knocked on their door. I heard barking. Yes!! They had two little terriers named Gracie and Garbo. For a two-dog walk, they were going to pay me one and a half times my regular rate.

So now I had five dogs to walk. That seemed like plenty. If I needed more, I could sign them up later.

I was sure I would be able to make enough money to buy excellent gifts for Mommy and Elizabeth by Mother's Day.

Little Sister

by Ann M. Martin
author of The Baby-sitters Club®

More Titles... ➡

The Baby-sitters Little Sister titles continued...

❑	MQ69188-0	#80	Karen's Christmas Tree	$2.99
❑	MQ69189-9	#81	Karen's Accident	$2.99
❑	MQ69190-2	#82	Karen's Secret Valentine	$3.50
❑	MQ69191-0	#83	Karen's Bunny	$3.50
❑	MQ69192-9	#84	Karen's Big Job	$3.50
❑	MQ69193-7	#85	Karen's Treasure	$3.50
❑	MQ69194-5	#86	Karen's Telephone Trouble	$3.50
❑	MQ06585-8	#87	Karen's Pony Camp	$3.50
❑	MQ06586-6	#88	Karen's Puppet Show	$3.50
❑	MQ06587-4	#89	Karen's Unicorn	$3.50
❑	MQ06588-2	#90	Karen's Haunted House	$3.50
❑	MQ06589-0	#91	Karen's Pilgrim	$3.50
❑	MQ06590-4	#92	Karen's Sleigh Ride	$3.50
❑	MQ06591-2	#93	Karen's Cooking Contest	$3.50
❑	MQ06592-0	#94	Karen's Snow Princess	$3.50
❑	MQ06593-9	#95	Karen's Promise	$3.50
❑	MQ06594-7	#96	Karen's Big Move	$3.50
❑	MQ06595-5	#97	Karen's Paper Route	$3.50
❑	MQ06596-3	#98	Karen's Fishing Trip	$3.50
❑	MQ49760-X	#99	Karen's Big City Mystery	$3.50
❑	MQ50051-1	#100	Karen's Book	$3.50
❑	MQ50053-8	#101	Karen's Chain Letter	$3.50
❑	MQ50054-6	#102	Karen's Black Cat	$3.50
❑	MQ50055-4	#103	Karen's Movie Star	$3.99
❑	MQ50056-2	#104	Karen's Christmas Carol	$3.99
❑	MQ50057-0	#105	Karen's Nanny	$3.99
❑	MQ50058-9	#106	Karen's President	$3.99
❑	MQ50059-7	#107	Karen's Copycat	$3.99
❑	MQ43647-3		Karen's Wish Super Special #1	$3.25
❑	MQ44834-X		Karen's Plane Trip Super Special #2	$3.25
❑	MQ44827-7		Karen's Mystery Super Special #3	$3.25
❑	MQ45644-X		Karen, Hannie, and Nancy The Three Musketeers Super Special #4	$2.95
❑	MQ45649-0		Karen's Baby Super Special #5	$3.50
❑	MQ46911-8		Karen's Campout Super Special #6	$3.25
❑	MQ55407-7		BSLS Jump Rope Pack	$5.99
❑	MQ73914-X		BSLS Playground Games Pack	$5.99
❑	MQ89735-7		BSLS Photo Scrapbook Book and Camera Pack	$9.99
❑	MQ47677-7		BSLS School Scrapbook	$2.95
❑	MQ13801-4		Baby-sitters Little Sister Laugh Pack	$6.99
❑	MQ26497-2		Karen's Summer Fill-In Book	$2.95

Available wherever you buy books, or use this order form.

Scholastic Inc., P.O. Box 7502, Jefferson City, MO 65102

Please send me the books I have checked above. I am enclosing $_____
(please add $2.00 to cover shipping and handling). Send check or money order – no cash or C.O.Ds please.

Name_____Birthdate_____

Address_____

City_____State/Zip_____

Please allow four to six weeks for delivery. Offer good in U.S.A. only. Sorry, mail orders are not available to residents of Canada. Prices subject to change.

BSLS998